Reading is ofte~~jER~~ primary grades. reading success.

When they rea rds: story and picture clues, ho elling relationships. The **Hello Reader!** *Phonics Fun* series focuses on sound/spelling relationships through phonics activities. Phonics instruction unlocks the door to understanding sounds and the letters or spelling patterns that represent them.

The **Hello Reader!** *Phonics Fun* series is divided into the following three sets of books, based on important phonic elements:

- **Sci-Fi Phonics**: word families
- **Monster Phonics**: consonants, blends, and digraphs
- **Funny Tale Phonics**: short and long vowels

Learn About Consonants

The Monster Phonics stories, including *Monster Town*, feature words that begin with the same sound. These books help children become aware of and use consonant sounds when decoding, or sounding out, new words. After reading the book, you might wish to begin lists of words that begin with the same sound. Your child can use these lists for reading practice or as reference when spelling words.

Enjoy the Activities

- Challenge your child to build words using the letters and word parts provided. Help your child by demonstrating how to sound out new words.
- Match words with pictures to help your child attach meaning to text.
- Become word detectives by identifying story words with the same beginning sound.
- Keep the activities game-like and praise your child's efforts.

Develop Fluency

Encourage your child to read these books again and again and again. Each time, set a different purpose for reading.

- Point to a word in the story. Say it aloud. Ask your child what sound he or she hears at the beginning of the word. Then look at the letter or letters that stand for that sound.
- Suggest to your child that he or she read the book to a friend, family member, or even a pet.

Whatever you do, have fun with the books and instill the joy of reading in your child. It is one of the most important things you can do!

— Wiley Blevins, Reading Specialist
Ed.M., Harvard University

To Mom with love
—J.B.S.

For Alan Tiegreen,
who inspired me in so many ways in my career
—N.E.

Text copyright © 1997 by Judith Bauer Stamper.
Illustrations copyright © 1997 by Nate Evans.
All rights reserved. Published by Scholastic Inc.
HELLO READER! and CARTWHEEL BOOKS and associated logos
are trademarks and/or registered trademarks of Scholastic Inc.

Library of Congress Cataloging-in-Publication Data

Stamper, Judith Bauer.
    Monster town / by Judith Bauer Stamper; illustrated by Nate Evans;
    phonics activities by Wiley Blevins.
        p.   cm.—(Hello reader! Phonics fun. Monster phonics)
    "Consonants: t, p, m, s."
    "Cartwheel Books."
    Summary: Little Monster goes to a strange new town where each day he is
introduced to a new letter. Includes related activities.
    ISBN 0-590-76265-6
    [1. Monsters—Fiction. 2. Alphabet—Fiction. 3. Stories in rhyme.]
I. Evans, Nate, ill. II. Blevins, Wiley. III. Title. IV. Series.
PZ8.3.S78255Mo   1997
[E]—dc21   97-14516
                                                                        CIP
                                                                        AC

10 9 8 7 6 5 4 3 2 1   7 8 9/9 0/0 01 02
                    Printed in the U.S.A.   24
                    First printing, November 1997

MonSter Town

by Judith Bauer Stamper
Illustrated by Nate Evans
Phonics Activities by Wiley Blevins

Hello Reader! Phonics Fun
Monster Phonics • Consonants: _t, p, m, s_

SCHOLASTIC INC.
New York   Toronto   London   Auckland   Sydney

We welcome you to Monster Town.

MONSTER TOWN

See big bad monsters
all around.

Tacos to eat,
T-shirts to wear,

Pizza, popcorn,
a pie to eat,

pink pigs, and penguins
are on the street.

Today is M day in Monster Town.

Look for M words all around.

Mud to play in,
music so nice.

Funny monkeys
race monster mice!

Today is S day in Monster Town.

Look for S words
all around.

A swing is super.
A seesaw is fun.

Play soccer in silly socks under the sun.

Learn your letter
for each day.

Then join the monsters
as they play,

on T day
and P day,

on M day
and S day...

and every day!

• PHONICS ACTIVITIES •
Which doesn't belong?
Point to the picture that doesn't begin with the same sound.

Build a Word

Use the letters in the monsters' T-shirts to make new words. Add each letter to the word ending. If it makes a word, say it aloud.

☐	en	☐	ad
☐	at	☐	ack
☐	op	☐	ell

Picture Match

Match the picture with its name. Find the picture's name in the story.

sun

trains

pigs

monkeys

socks

toads

Monster's Mom

Help the monster find his mom. The monster can only use the path with objects whose names begin with <u>m</u>.

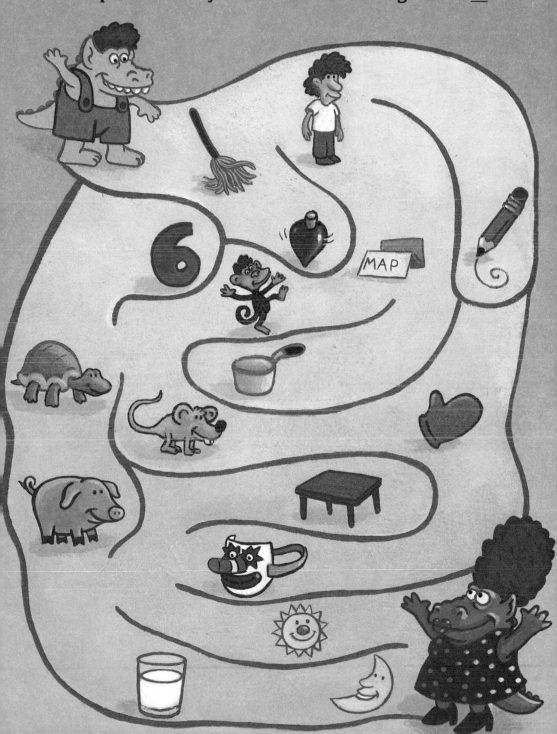

Answers

Which doesn't belong?

Build a Word

pen, pat, pop, pad, pack;
men, mat, mop, mad;
sat, sop, sad, sack, sell;
ten, top, tad, tack, tell

Picture Match

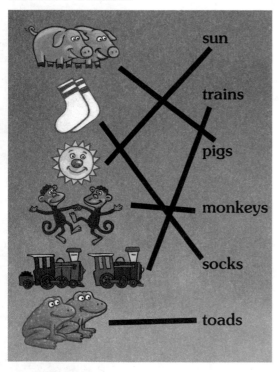

Monster Mom